FIELD TRIP TO MARS

BY JEFF DINARDO
ILLUSTRATED BY DAVE CLEGG

RED CHAIR PRESS

Funny Bone Books

and Funny Bone Readers are produced and published by
Red Chair Press LLC   PO Box 333   South Egremont, MA 01258-0333
www.redchairpress.com

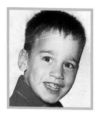

About the Author

Jeff Dinardo's books are filled with humor and silliness that captures a child's imagination. When not writing, Jeff runs a successful design firm specializing in textbooks for use in classrooms from K-8.

About the Artist

Dave Clegg lives and works on a small horse farm in north Georgia with his wife Lyn. All of Dave's work is done digitally on his computer. When he is not drawing, he can be found creating songs with his guitar or making robot sculptures!

Publisher's Cataloging-In-Publication Data
Names: Dinardo, Jeffrey. | Clegg, Dave, illustrator.
Title: The Jupiter twins. Book 1, Field trip to Mars / by Jeff Dinardo ; illustrated by Dave Clegg.
Other Titles: Field trip to Mars

Description: South Egremont, MA : Red Chair Press, [2018] | Series: Funny bone books. First chapters | Interest age level: 005-007. | Summary: "Trudy and Tina are best friends. They are also twins. Trudy loves adventure and Tina is happy to go along for the ride--as long as it is a smooth ride! Today the class is going on a field trip to Mars. Enjoy the fun on the Red Planet. First Chapters books are easy introductions to exploring longer text."--Provided by publisher.

Identifiers: LCCN 2017934021 | ISBN 978-1-63440-249-1 (library hardcover) | ISBN 978-1-63440-253-8 (paperback) | ISBN 978-1-63440-257-6 (ebook)

Subjects: LCSH: Twins--Juvenile fiction. | Mars (Planet)--Juvenile fiction. | Outer space--Exploration--Juvenile fiction. | School field trips--Juvenile fiction. | CYAC: Twins--Fiction. | Mars (Planet)--Fiction. | Outer space--Exploration--Fiction. | School field trips--Fiction.

Classification: LCC PZ7.D6115 Juf 2018 (print) | LCC PZ7.D6115 (ebook) | DDC [E]--dc23

Printed in Canada

102017 1P FRNS18

CONTENTS

1 BORED 5

2 WHO IS THIS? 12

3 WE ARE IN TROUBLE 16

4 UP AND OUT 22

Meet the Characters

TRUDY

TINA

Ms. Bickleblorb

Spot

🚀 1 BORED

All the kids got off the space bus.

"Please stay with your partners," said their teacher, Ms. Bickleblorb. "Have fun exploring Mars. But be careful!" she added.

Trudy and Tina were partners, as always.

They were also twins.

"Bored!" yawned Trudy as she kicked a Mars rock with her foot.

"I hope it doesn't rain," said Tina.

Some students went to collect rocks. Others went to hike a nearby mountain. Trudy and Tina just sat on the red dirt.

Trudy took out her phone from her backpack. "Ugg," she said. "No signal on Mars!"

"I wish we were home on Jupiter," said Tina.

Just then the ground under them started to shake and tremble.

"Goodness!" they shouted as they looked at each other.

A hole in the red soil started to open next to them.

The hole got wider and wider.

Trudy and Tina just had time to grab each other before they fell through the hole and were gone.

"Get off me!" said Trudy as she pushed her sister off her back. They had fallen quite far but landed safely on the soft ground.

"We can't get out the way we came," said Tina as she dusted herself off.

"Ms. Bickleblorb said to explore," added Trudy. "So let's explore!"

WHO IS THIS?

They had not gone far when they heard someone or something crying.

"Let's go back the way we came," said Tina nervously.

"Nonsense," said Trudy. "Nothing scares me!"

Around the next curve they saw a tiny creature sobbing.

"Ewwww!" said Tina. "That looks yucky!"

Trudy went over and gently picked up the tiny alien. It instantly stopped crying and smiled at her. The creature licked her face with its purple tongue.

"Oh isn't he precious?" Trudy said. "I'll name him Spot!"

"You can't keep him!" said Tina.

Trudy ignored her sister. She let Spot ride in her backpack with its head sticking out.

Soon the tunnel ended.

"Rats," said Tina "We are still stuck down here."

They tried other paths, but every tunnel they took ended the same way. There was no way out!

3 WE ARE IN TROUBLE

MUNCH, MUNCH, MUNCH.

A loud munching sound was coming from behind them and getting closer. "What do we do?" cried Tina.

An ugly, green monster with giant teeth
was munching its way right toward them.

"*HELP!*" shouted Tina.

Trudy reached into her backpack and
pulled out her notebook. She also gave
Spot a quick snuggle.

"I think we read about these guys in
school," she said.

"*HURRY!*" said Tina. "Before we get
eaten!"

Trudy flipped through pages of
her book. "Humm, that's not it," she said
calmly. "Maybe it was near the end?"

"*WE ARE GOING TO GET
SQUISHED!*" shouted Tina, who was
frantically trying to climb out of the way.
The monster was getting closer.

"Ah, here it is!" said Trudy as she
pointed to a picture in the book.

"It's a Mars Rock Muncher," she said.
"He is quite gentle... unless you are a
rock."

The monster was right at their heels.

"Follow me!" said Trudy. Then she jumped in the air and landed on the monster's back as he passed them by.

"Wait for me!" Tina shouted as she closed her eyes and jumped on too.

The Mars Rock Muncher didn't pay them any attention. But when he got to the end of the tunnel those giant munching teeth started eating a hole right through the rock.

"Jumping Jupiter!" shouted Trudy with a laugh. "Hang on!"

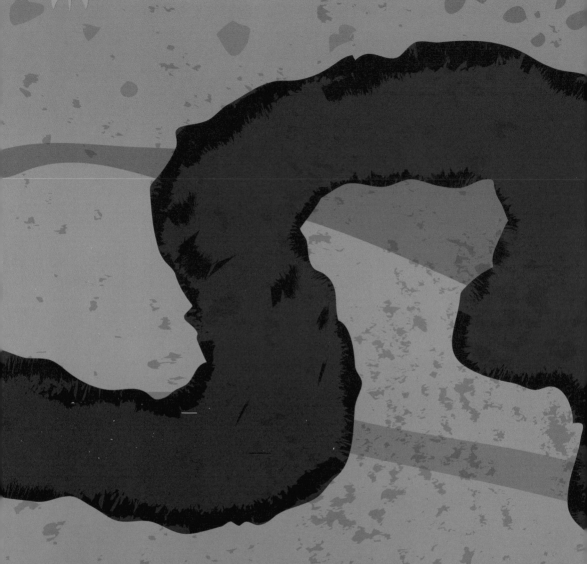

They hung on tight as the monster dug
a tunnel left, then right, then down.
Finally he turned and headed straight up!
"Here we go!" said Trudy.

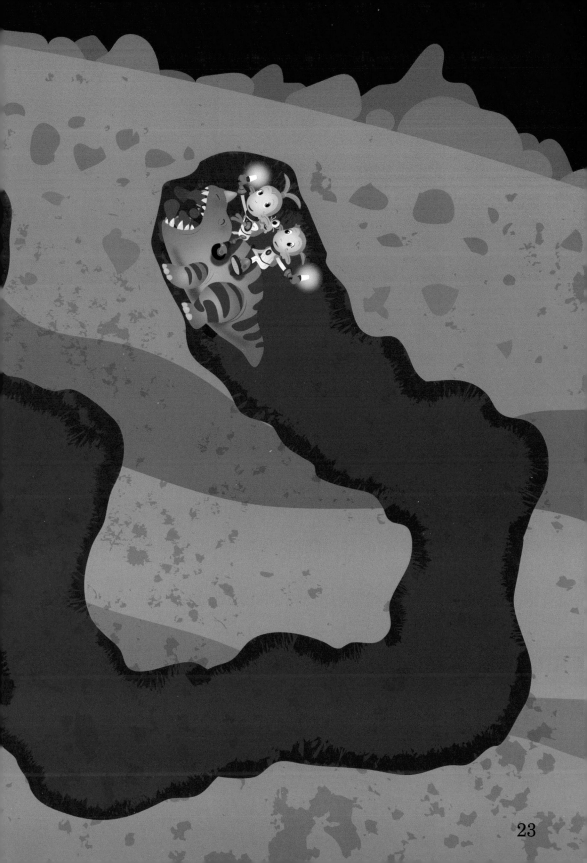

They broke through to the surface
of the planet.

The Jupiter twins hopped off.

Trudy smiled but Tina could barely
stand on her own two legs.

They were just in time to see the space bus with their teacher and fellow students being sucked into the mouth of a giant jelly-like alien.

"That doesn't look good," said Trudy.

Tina nearly fainted.

"There is something familiar about that alien," said Trudy as she reached into her backpack for her notebook again.

Just then, Spot jumped out and started running right toward the alien.

"Blip. Blap. Bloop," he shouted.

Once the giant alien saw Spot, she
spit out the space bus.

PITOOEY

"Bloopykins," she roared as she scooped
Spot up.

"It's Spot's mother!" said Trudy.
"That's why Spot must have been crying."
    The mother alien slid away smiling
with Spot riding on her back.
    Trudy looked sad.
    Tina put her arm around her sister.
"Spot will be happier now," she said.

Ms. Bickleblorb scraped the alien goo off the bus and waved to the twins. "Hop aboard girls," she called.

The space bus rocketed off into space, heading back home to Jupiter.

That night Trudy was sad.

"I miss Spot," she said.

Tina gave Trudy a present.

It was a picture she drew of

her sister holding Spot.

Trudy was happy again.